Wibble Wobble

For Finn

MM

For my Mum and best friend -
thanks for EVERYTHING

JM

ISBN 0-439-39017-6

Published by Scholastic Inc., 557 Broadway, New York, NY 10012,
by arrangement with Tiger Tales, an imprint of ME Media LLC.

12 11 10 4 5 6 7 8/0

Printed in the U.S.A. 40

First Scholastic printing, January 2003

Wibble Wobble

by Miriam Moss

illustrated by Joanna Mockler

SCHOLASTIC INC.
New York Toronto London Auckland Sydney
Mexico City New Delhi Hong Kong Buenos Aires

All William ever wanted in the whole world was to have a loose tooth.

Everyone else in his class had one.
Louie's twisted round and round
and Rosa's lay flat on its back.

But William's teeth seemed stuck,
superglued to his gums.

"It isn't fair," said William. "Everyone else at school tells loose tooth stories."

"Sammy swallowed his...

Rosa's fell
down the toilet...

and Louie's flew out
when he scored a goal!"

"When your loose tooth comes out, Grandma," said William, "you get a silver dollar from the Tooth Fairy."

"Is that so?" said Grandma.

"Yes," said William. "And if it comes out at school, you have to keep it somewhere safe."

William continued, "Vicky tied hers into the knot in her shoelaces...

and Martin hid his in a cotton ball in his ear.

AND...

today Jasmine's got lost up her nose. Mrs. King said she'd keep them safe from now on."

The next day during quiet time, William felt one of his teeth move at last!

"Mrs. King!" he cried. "My tooth moved! I felt it!"

William pushed his tooth forward with his tongue then sucked it back for Mrs. King to see.

"Look, Rosa!" he said.

"Look, Louie!"

Push, pull,
jiggle, joggle.

Poke, flick,
wibble,
wobble.

"Come on, William," called Mom at bedtime. "How long does it take you to brush your teeth?"

"A long time," said William. "It hurts my loose tooth."

William just couldn't leave his loose tooth alone.

Push, pull, jiggle, joggle.
Poke, flick, wibble,
wobble.

"Look, Louie," said William the next day, twisting his tooth round and round. "Look, Rosa," he said, as it lay flat on its back.

By bedtime William's tooth was hanging by one thin little thread.

push, pull,
poke, flick,

jiggle, joggle.
wibble, wobble.

Suddenly, the tooth flipped upside down and got stuck!

"Ow! Ow!" yelled William, jumping out of bed. "Mom! Dad!" he cried, rushing downstairs.

Gently Dad turned the tooth back right-side up.

"Why doesn't it just come out?" said William.

"Don't worry," said Dad. "It will."

In gym class the next day William did his best somersault ever. And when he stood up, his tooth was sitting on his tongue! William took it out and looked at it. It was so tiny!

"I'll look after it until you go home," said Mrs. King, wrapping it in a tissue and putting it on top of the filing cabinet.

"Then can I take it home?" asked William, feeling a bit wobbly himself.

"Of course," said Mrs. King.

That afternoon, William sat poking his tongue into the hole in his gum, waiting for Louie to finish his art project.

Suddenly Louie shouted, "Aaargh!" and started dancing about. "I've got paint in my eye!"

"I'll get a tissue, Mrs. King," said Rosa.

Mrs. King dabbed Louie's eye. By the time Louie was cleaned up, it was time to go home.

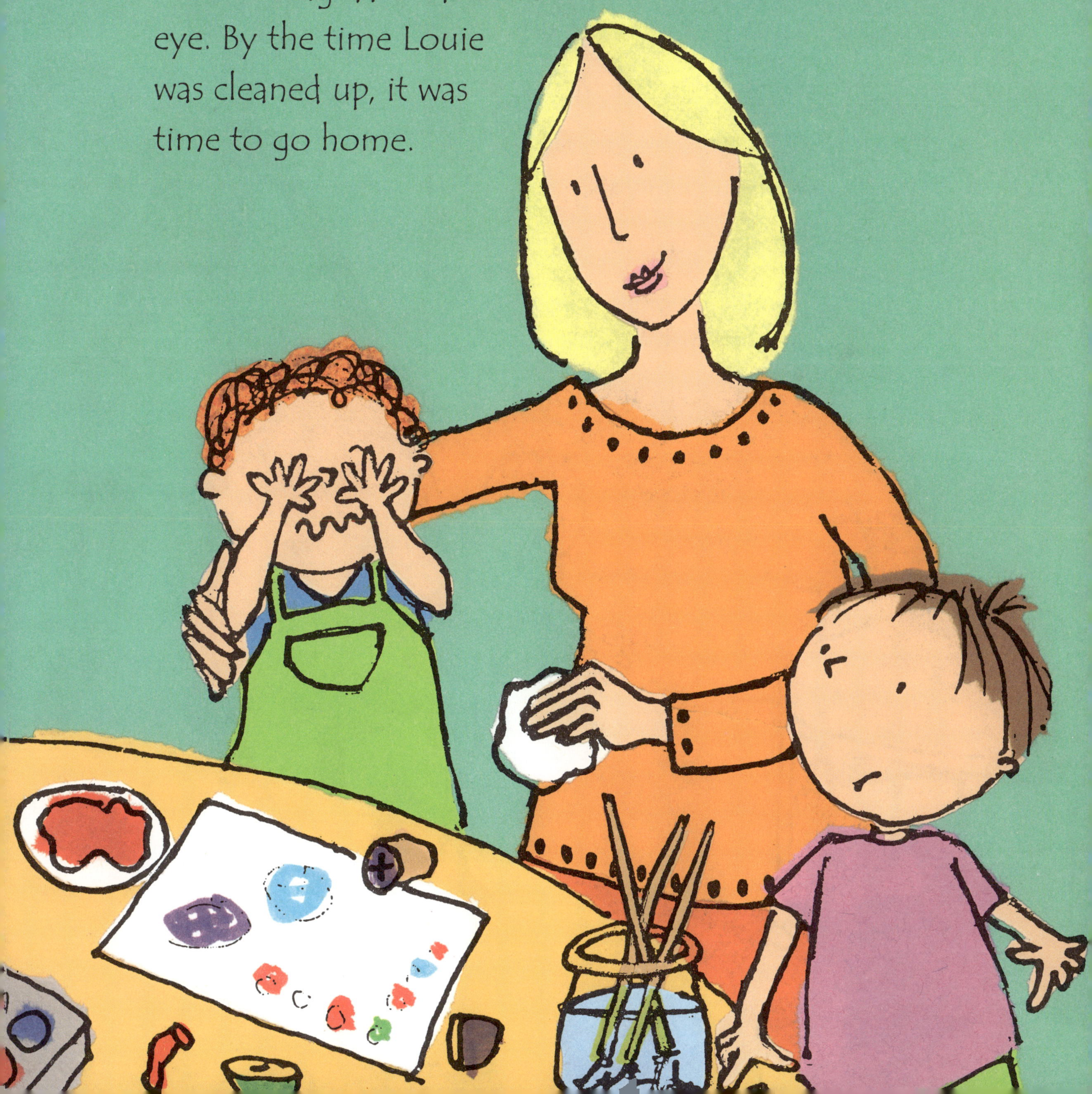

"Look, Mom!" William said. "My tooth came out!"

"Oh, William!" said Mom. "Where is it?"

"It's on the filing cabinet, wrapped up in a tissue," said William.

"Here it is," said Mrs. King. Then she said, "Oh, it's gone."

They searched everywhere. Suddenly William stopped.

"Rosa gave Louie a tissue," he said, "when he got red paint in his eye."

Mom and Mrs. King looked at each other.

"Don't worry William," said Mom,
searching in the wastebasket. "We'll find it."

William sat down and stared at his feet. He was missing his tooth very much by now. He was sure they'd never find it.

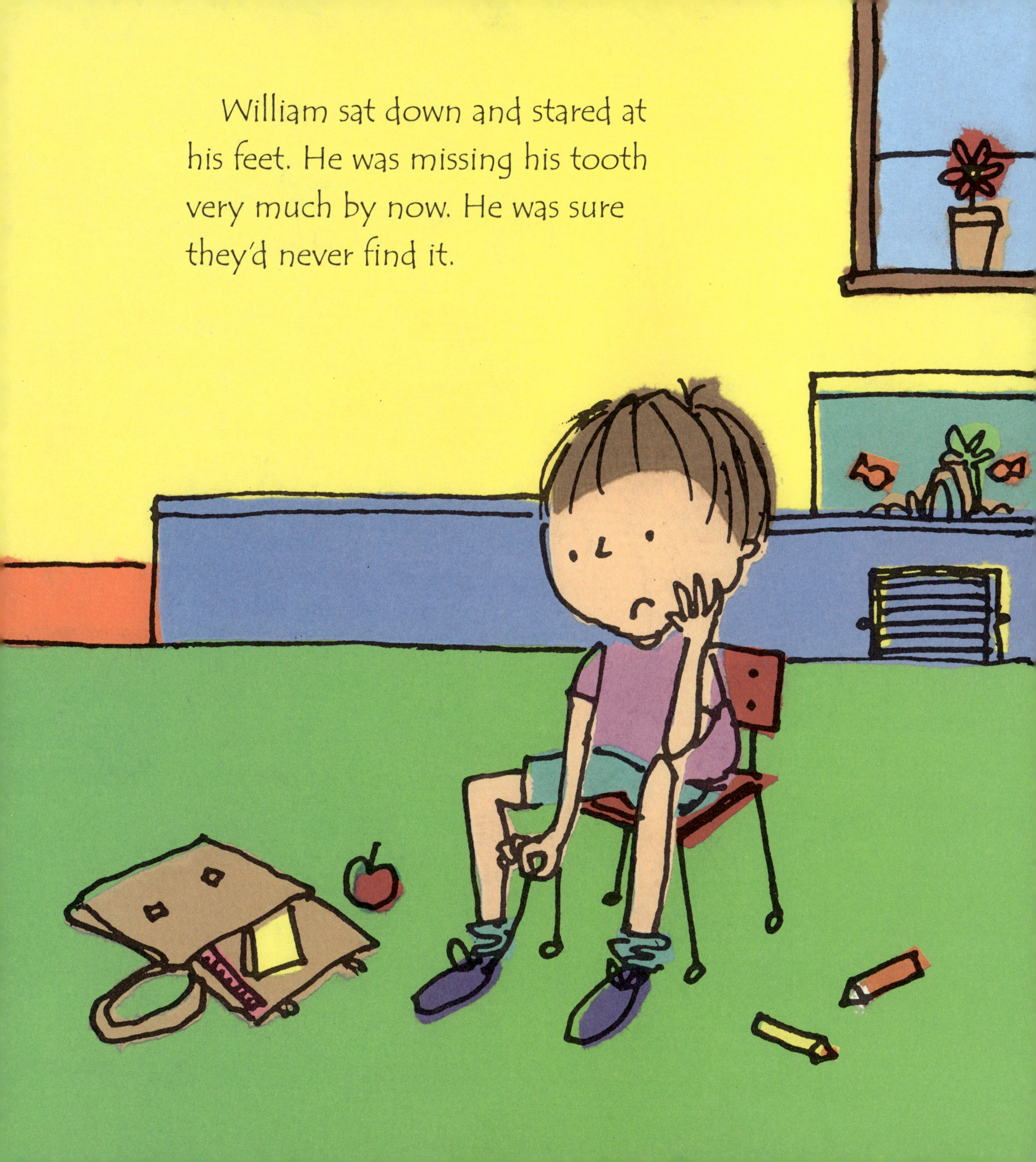

Suddenly, Mom stood up. "This might be it!" She unwrapped a tissue—and there was

William's tooth!

Mrs. King washed the tooth and gave it back to William.

"Perhaps the Tooth Fairy will leave something special tonight," said Mrs. King. "After all that."

The next morning William looked under his pillow. There lay a little wooden box. He lifted the lid and inside was a shiny silver dollar!

When William got to school he told everyone his loose tooth story.

"I would think you'd like a rest from loose teeth for a while, William!" said Mrs. King.

"Yes," said William. "I would!"

On the way home from school, William took his silver dollar and bought an enormous ice cream.

It had little colored candies stuck all over it, layers of chocolate, and chewy toffee in the middle.

William unwrapped it and took a big bite.

Ping!

went the little colored candies.

Crack!

went the chocolate.

Squish!

went the ice cream.

Crunch!

went the ice-cold, rock-hard toffee . . . and guess what?

Another tooth wiggled!

Push, pull, jiggle, joggle.

poke, flick,

wibble,

wobble.